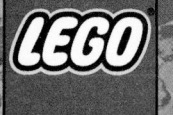

LEGO NINJAGO

Masters of Spinjitzu

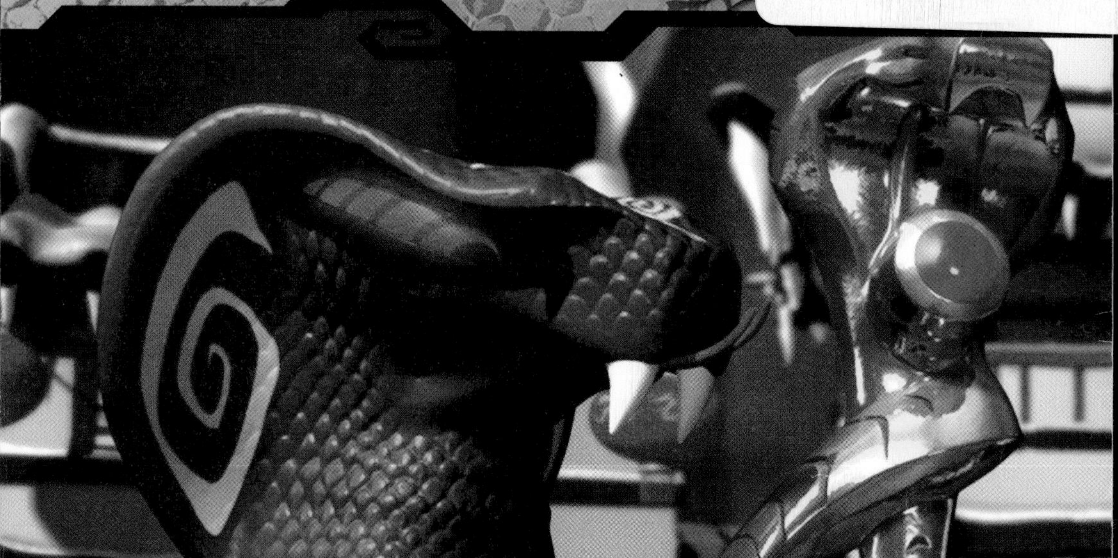

RISE OF THE SNAKES

ADAPTED BY TRACEY WEST

SCHOLASTIC INC.
NEW YORK TORONTO LONDON AUCKLAND
SYDNEY MEXICO CITY NEW DELHI HONG KONG

ISBN 978-0-545-43592-5

12 11 10 9 8 7 6 5 4 3 2 1   12 13 14 15 16 17/0

Printed in the U.S.A.   40

First printing, May 2012

TRAINING DAY

"Let's do it! Hiii-yah!"

Sensei Wu heard the sound of ninja training echo through the dojo. But the training room was empty. Puzzled, Sensei Wu opened the door to the dojo's parlor.

Cole, Zane, Jay, and Kai weren't training. They were playing a ninja video game!

Sensei Wu unplugged the game.

"Just because Lord Garmadon escaped doesn't mean he won't return," Sensei Wu told them. "You must keep up with your training."

"We can train tomorrow," Cole said.

"Never put off until tomorrow what can be done today," Sensei Wu said.

Cole smiled. "Then I guess I'll eat this pizza today."

"No pizza!" Sensei Wu yelled. "In order to reach your full potential, you must train!"

"Don't worry, master," said Zane. "We'll be ready when Lord Garmadon returns."

Kai's sister, Nya, ran into the room.

"Guys! Lord Garmadon has returned!" she cried.

The ninja quickly grabbed the four Golden Weapons of Spinjitzu. Kai held the Sword of Fire. Cole held the Scythe of Quakes. Zane held the Shurikens of Ice. Jay held the Nunchuks of Lightning.

Then each ninja climbed onto his dragon, and they streaked through the sky to the village.

CRASH LANDING

The ninja were a little out of practice. They came to a crash landing in Jamanakai Village. The frightened villagers were screaming and running into their homes.

A tall, black shadow loomed over the village. Lord Garmadon!

Quickly, the ninja ran to face him. They drew their Weapons.

A figure in black stepped forward. But it wasn't Lord Garmadon, it was a little boy.

"It is I — Lloyd Garmadon!" he cried.

"He must be Lord Garmadon's son," Cole realized.

"Give me your candy, or I'll release the Serpentine on you!" Lloyd threatened. He opened a jar, and toy snakes sprang out.

"Does he really think he can scare people with an old bedtime story?" Kai asked.

"The Serpentine are real, Kai," Zane said seriously.

"Yeah, right," Kai said. "So, I'm supposed to believe an ancient race of snake people that used to rule Ninjago are now locked underground?"

The ninja didn't take Lloyd seriously. They hung him by his pants from a sign in town.

"I will get my revenge on you all!" Lloyd yelled.

The ninja just laughed. Zane bought some candy, and they ate it in front of Lloyd.

"*Mmm*, cotton candy," Jay said, taking a big bite.

THE PROPHECY

The ninja went back to their dragons. As Kai climbed aboard his, a scroll fell out of a bag attached to the saddle.

"That's Sensei's bag," Zane said. "You must have taken it by accident."

Zane read from the scroll. It revealed a prophecy about the future.

"One ninja will rise above the others and become the Green Ninja, the ninja destined to defeat the dark lord," Zane read.

"You think they mean Lord Garmadon?" Cole asked.

They looked at the scroll. Besides the green ninja, there were four other ninja: one red, one blue, one black, and one white.

"Wait a minute. Is that us?" Kai asked.

"Is anyone else thinking what I'm thinking?" Kai asked.

"Like how good I'm going to look in green?" Jay replied.

"Technically, *I* am the best," Zane pointed out.

Cole got angry. "Everyone, stop it! We're a team, remember? We weren't even supposed to see this scroll. Let's go back and train."

While the ninja flew back to the dojo, Lloyd stomped through the snowy mountains.

"Stupid ninja! I'll show them!" he said, kicking the rocks at his feet.

Clang! One of the rocks hit something hard. Curious, Lloyd pushed away the snow. He found a stone with strange carvings on it.

Lloyd pulled a lever, and the stone began to slide open!

THE SERPENTINE

"Aaaaaah!"

Lloyd stumbled and fell through the hole down into an icy chamber. He stood up — and then he heard a creepy voice behind him.

"You are out of your mind to travel *sssso* far away from home, little one."

Lloyd gasped. A *real* Serpentine slithered toward him!

"Look into my *eyesss*," the snake creature hissed, and his eyes glowed red. "I will control your mind."

Terrified, Lloyd stepped backward. He ducked to avoid the Serpentine's hypnotizing eyes.

Lloyd had backed into a column of ice. The Serpentine saw his own reflection in the ice. He had hypnotized himself by mistake!

Lloyd grinned. "No. I will control *you* from now on!"

Lloyd didn't know it yet, but he had control of a Serpentine general, the leader of the Hypnobrai tribe.

"What will you have *usss* do, *massster*?" the general hissed.

As he spoke, the Hypnobrai soldiers marched out of the shadows.

"My own army of snakes!" Lloyd yelled. "*Mwahahahaha!*"

A LITTLE FRIENDLY COMPETITION

Back at the dojo, the four ninja decided to hold a tournament.

"Last one standing is the Green Ninja!" Kai exclaimed.

First Kai and Jay faced off. But neither ninja could control his Golden Weapon. Jay got a shock from his own Nunchuks. And Kai's Sword shot out energy blasts when he didn't expect it. But Kai still managed to win.

"Ninjago!" Kai cried, and Cole and Zane began to battle. At first, Cole couldn't control his Scythe. Zane tried to freeze him in place with the power of his Shurikens. But Cole knocked down Zane for the win.

Now it was Cole against Kai. Who would win?

But they never found out — because Kai's Sword set the training room on fire!

Sensei Wu arrived just in time. He used the Shurikens of Ice to put out the fire.

"What were you thinking?" he asked angrily.

"We want to know . . . which one of us is the chosen one?" Kai asked.

"None of you," Sensei Wu replied, "if you don't unlock your full potential! None of you are near the level of the Green Ninja."

NYA'S DISCOVERY

While Sensei scolded the boys, Nya was visiting Jamanakai Village. Suddenly, she heard villagers screaming.

Lloyd Garmadon marched through the town, followed by the Hypnobrai army. The general and Scales, his second-in-command, stood at his side.

"Take the candy! Take it all!" Lloyd yelled.

Nya quickly hid behind a building. She watched the general, who held a golden staff. His red eyes began to glow and spin. He hypnotized all the villagers.

Nya listened as Scales argued with the general.

"Why are we raiding a town just to get sweets?" Scales asked.

"You will do as I say, because I hold the staff!" the general replied.

Back at the dojo, Sensei Wu had a vision of the village. He ran to the training room.

"The Serpentine are back!" he told the ninja. "Everyone in Jamanakai Village is in danger!"

RESCUE MISSION

The ninja hurried to their dragons and flew back to the village. They found Lloyd pushing a wheelbarrow full of candy.

"Sorry, Little Garmadon, but it's past your bedtime!" Kai said.

Lloyd scowled. He turned to his army. "Get them!" he yelled.

"*Sssseize them!*" the general hissed.

The Hypnobrai army and the hypnotized villagers surrounded the four ninja. Jay twirled his Nunchuks, ready to fight.

"No! The Weapons are too unstable!" Zane warned.

"I guess that leaves us with . . . RUN!" Jay yelled.

The ninja ran into Nya.

"They've hypnotized everyone in town," she told them. "When you hear them rattle their tails, don't look them in the eyes!"

"How are we going to fight them with our eyes closed?" Jay asked.

"We need to get the staff from the general," Nya said. "It holds the antivenom. We can use it to break the spell on the villagers."

The ninja split up and raced off to find the general. Kai was quickly surrounded by Hypnobrai soldiers.

"Wanna play?" he asked them. "How about a little Spinjitzu? *Ninjaaaago!*"

Kai began to spin, becoming a twirling tornado of red energy. But he was so out of practice that he couldn't control his path. He slammed into a wall!

Zane saw Lloyd escaping with the candy. He threw his Shurikens in front of Lloyd, and they froze the ground in his path. Lloyd stopped short, and the candy tumbled out of his wheelbarrow.

"We should have dealt with you the first time," Zane said.

"Retreat!" Lloyd cried.

THE POWER OF THE SNAKES

The Serpentine army tried to flee the village. But Cole stopped the general with a high kick. The staff fell to the ground. Cole picked it up.

The general ran away, but Scales stood his ground. "Look into my *eyessssss*," he hissed. "I control you."

"Cole!" Nya cried. She ran between Cole and Scales. Then she jumped up and kicked the snake creature.

Scales hurried away. Nya pointed to the staff in Cole's hands.

"You have the antivenom!" she yelled. "Quick, the fountain!"

Cole jumped onto the big fountain in the center of the village. He placed the staff in the water, and a blue mist rose up. The villagers breathed it in. Soon they were back to normal.

Sensei Wu walked through the mist.

"We're sorry, Sensei," Kai told him. "If we had dealt with Lloyd before he became a problem, none of this would have happened."

"Even lessons learned the hard way are lessons learned," Sensei Wu replied kindly. Then he grew serious. "A great evil has been released. I fear troubling times are coming."

That trouble was brewing deep in the tomb of the Hypnobrai.

"I hold the key to destroying the ninja!" Scales bragged. His eyes glowed red.

Back in the dojo, Cole's eyes glowed red, too. Scales still controlled Cole . . . and when the time was ready, he would strike.